Little Red Riding Hood

Key sound short oo spellings: o, oo, oul, u
Secondary sounds: ee, long oo, ou

Written by Nick Page
Illustrated by Clare Fennell

Reading with phonics

How to use this book

The **Reading with phonics** series helps you to have fun with your child and to support their learning of phonics and reading. It is aimed at children who have learned the letter sounds and are building confidence in their reading.

Each title in the series focuses on a different key sound. The entertaining retelling of the story repeats this sound frequently, and the different spellings for the sound are highlighted in red type. The first activity at the back of the book provides practice in reading and using words that contain this sound. The key sound for **Little Red Riding Hood** is the **short oo**.

Start by reading the story to your child, asking them to join in with the refrain in bold. Next, encourage them to read the story with you. Give them a hand to decode tricky words.

Now look at the activity pages at the back of the book. These are intended for you and your child to enjoy together. Most are not activities to complete in pencil or pen, but by reading and talking or pointing.

The **Key sound** pages focus on one sound, and on the various different groups of letters that produce that sound. Encourage your child to read the different letter groups and complete the activity, so they become more aware of the variety of spellings there are for the same sound.

The **Letters together** pages look at three pairs or groups of letters and at the sounds they make as they work together. Help your child to read the words and trace the route on the word maps.

Rhyme is used a lot in these retellings. Whatever stage your child has reached in their learning of phonics, it is always good practice for them to listen carefully for sounds and find words that rhyme. The pages on **Rhyming words** take six words from the story and ask children to read and find other words that rhyme with them.

The **Sight words** pages focus on a number of sight words that occur regularly but can nonetheless be challenging. Many of these words are not sounded out following the rules of phonics and the easiest thing is for children to learn them by sight, so that they do not worry about decoding them. These pages encourage children to retell the story, practicing sight words as they do so.

The **Picture dictionary** page asks children to focus closely on nine words from the story. Encourage children to look carefully at each word, cover it with their hand, write it on a separate piece of paper, and finally, check it!

Do not complete all the activities at once – doing one each time you read will ensure that your child continues to enjoy the stories and the time you are spending together. **Have fun!**

Here's a house, close to the wood.
Here's a girl who's kind and good.
Here's her favorite riding hood,
a gift from Grannie Annie.

In the woods, look out! Look out!
Could there be a wolf about?

"Grannie's ill," mom says, "so please, be a good girl, take some cheese, a book to read, some herbal teas and pudding to your grannie."

In the woods, look out! Look out!
Could there be a wolf about?

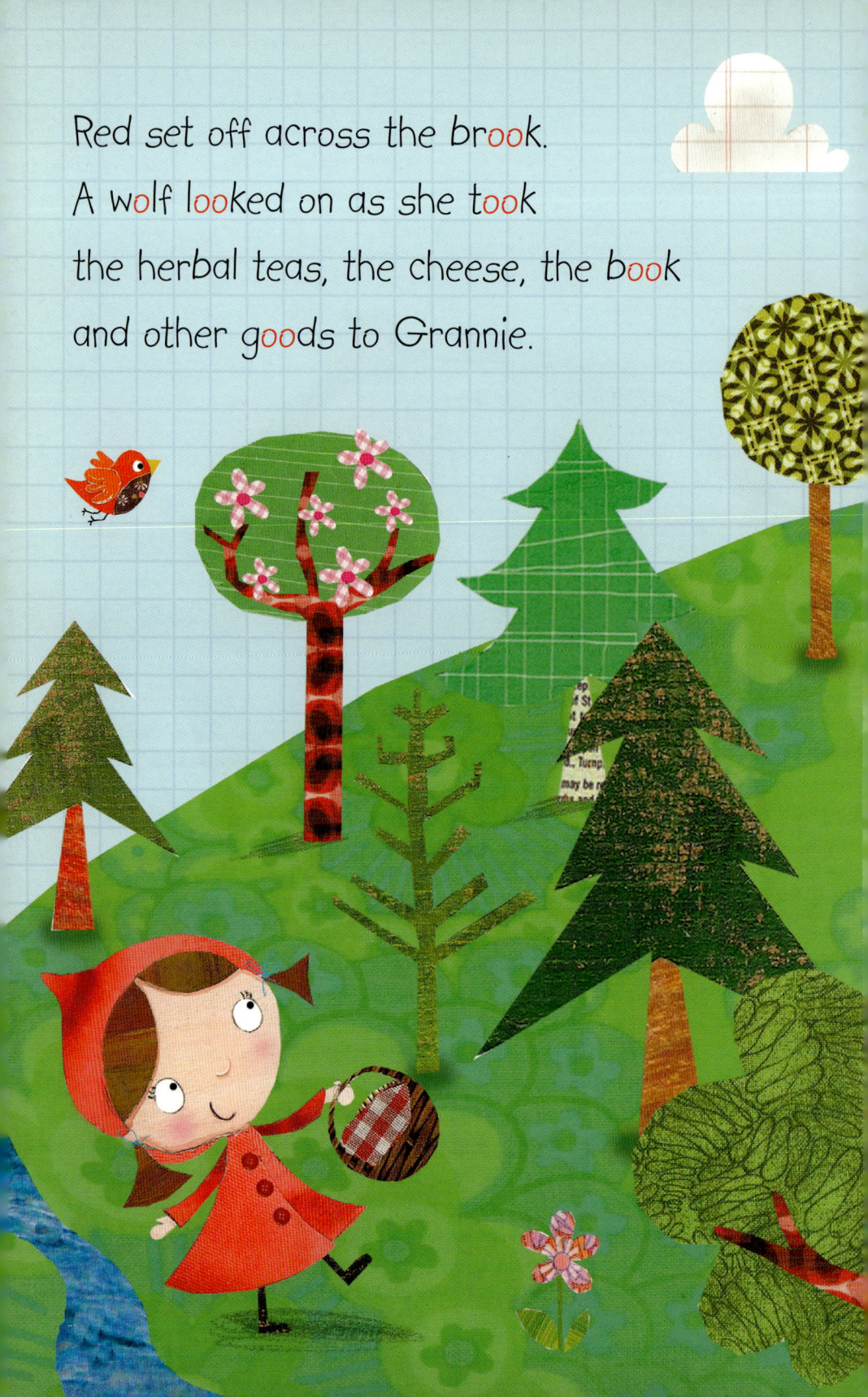

Red set off across the brook.
A wolf looked on as she took
the herbal teas, the cheese, the book
and other goods to Grannie.

In the woods, look out! Look out!
Could there be a wolf about?

Wolf says, "Yum! I have a hunch,
by hook or crook, this could be lunch."
He runs ahead and with one "CRUNCH,"
he swallows Grannie Annie.

In the woods, look out! Look out!
Could there be a wolf about?

Footsteps! Quick! Here comes Red.
Wolfie swiftly jumps in bed,
puts on Annie's clothes and says,
"Come and kiss your grannie!"

In the woods, look out! Look out!
Could there be a wolf about?

Red suspects a crooked plot.
"Grannie, what big ears you've got!"
"All the better to hear a lot,
now come and KISS your grannie!"

Grannie!

In the woods, look out! Look out!
Could there be a wolf about?

"Grannie, you've got such big eyes!"
"All the better to play I spy!"
(He's pulled the wool across her eyes.)
"Now COME AND KISS your grannie!"

Grannie!

In the woods, look out! Look out!
Could there be a wolf about?

Little Red, she sh**oo**k with fear:
"What big teeth you have! Oh, dear!"
"Better to eat you! Now, come here,
BECAUSE I'M THE W**O**LF –
NOT GRANNIE!"

Oh, dear!

In the w**oo**ds, l**oo**k out! L**oo**k out!
C**ou**ld there be a w**o**lf about?

A lumberjack was passing through.
He heard the scream, knew what to do,
rushed in and chopped the wolf in two,
and out popped Grannie Annie!

In the woods, look out! Look out!
Could there be a wolf about?

Grannie!

So ends the book of Riding Hood.
We hope it's clearly understood:
you must be careful in the wood
and please be good to Grannie!

In the woods, look out! Look out!
Could there be a wolf about?

Key sound

There are several different groups of letters that make the **short oo** sound. Practice them by looking at the words in Little Red's baskets and using them to make sentences. Can you use each word in a different sentence?

wood
good
book
hood
crooked
look
brook
took
goods
hook
shook
stood
wool
understood

Letters together

Look at these pairs of letters and say the sounds they make.

ee   **oo**   **ou**

Follow the words that contain **ee** to see Grannie's big teeth.

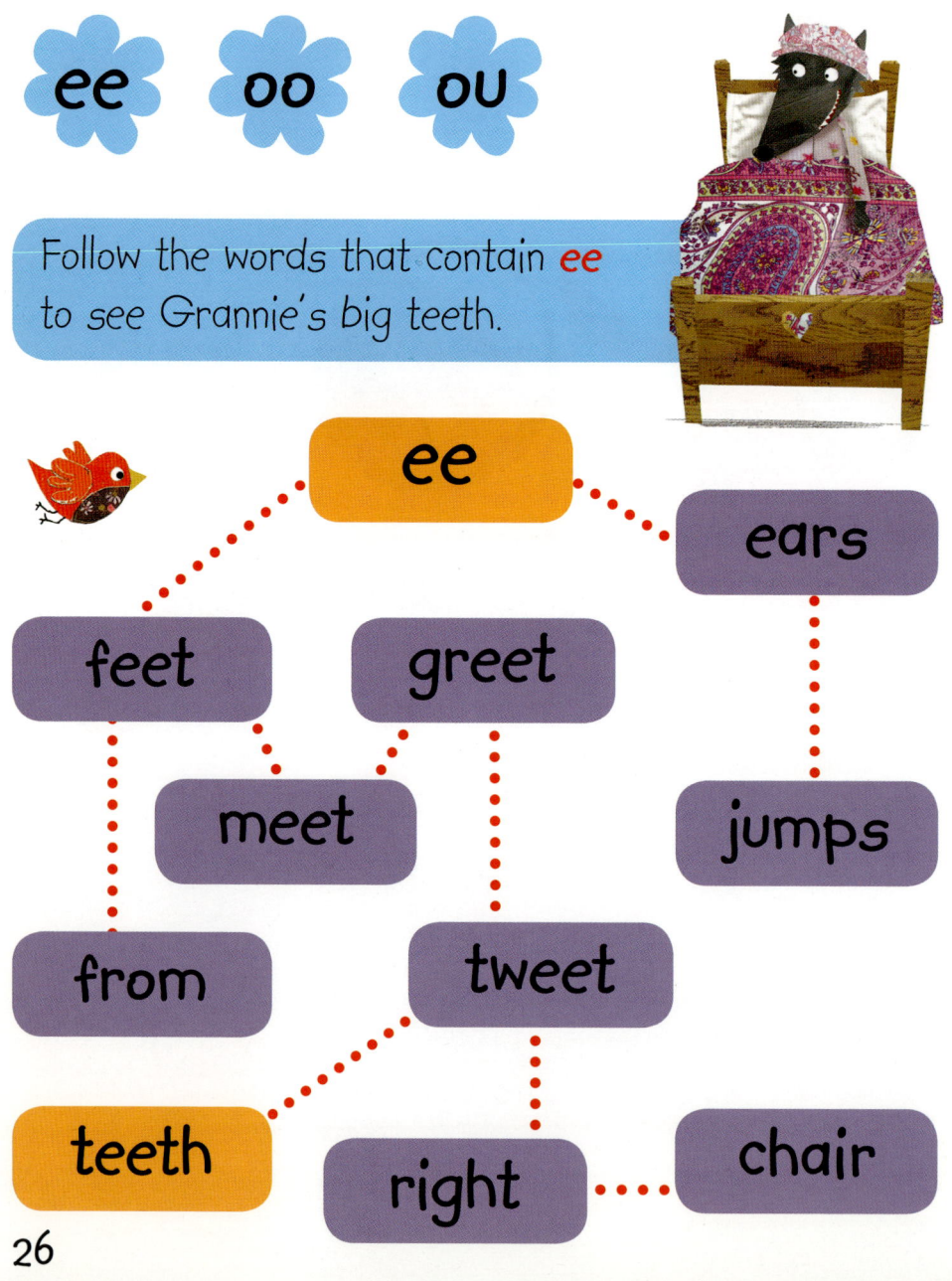

ee

feet   greet   ears

meet   jumps

from   tweet

teeth   right   chair

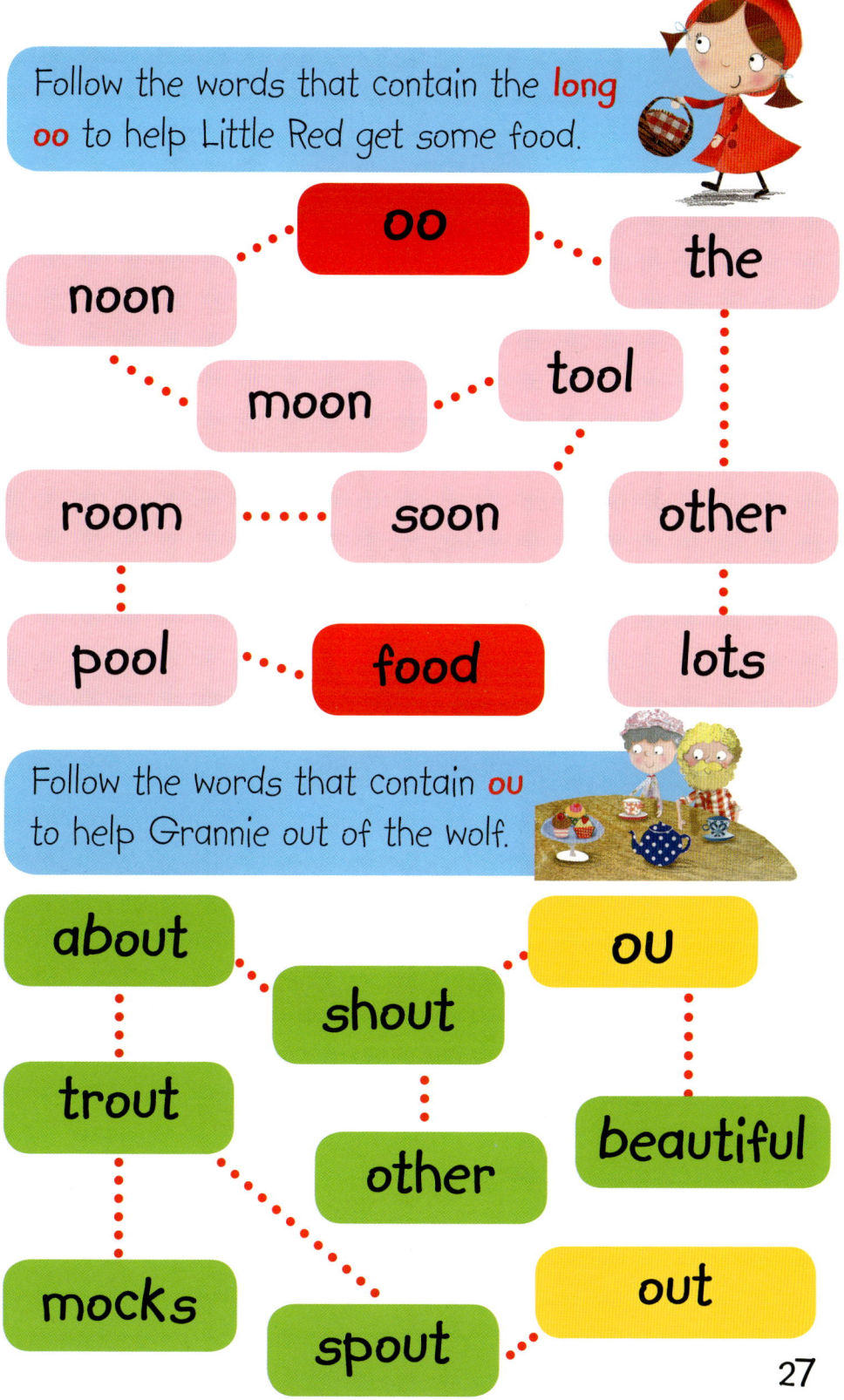

Rhyming words

Read the words in the flowers and point to other words that rhyme with them.

wolf	cook
brook	tea

book

bed	near
teeth	fear

hear

kiss	hood
red	fed

bed

Sight words

Many common words can be difficult to sound out. Practice them by reading these sentences about the story. Now make more sentences using other sight words from around the border.

Little Red's mom told her to **go** to see her grannie.

Red saw it was **the** wolf, not grannie!

Red took **some** food to Grannie Annie.

Grannie **lived** in the woods.

There was a wolf watching Little Red.

not • found • into • the

• morning • different • took • looked • had • there • with

Picture dictionary

Look carefully at the pictures and the words. Now cover the words, one at a time. Can you remember how to write them?

book

brook

cheese

ears

girl

grannie

hood

lumberjack

teeth